MRS TOGGLE'S ZIP

Magi Publications

Robin Pulver

MRS TOGGLE'S ZIP

Illustrated by R. W. Alley

Magi Publications, London

~~~~~~~~~~~~~~~~~~

For Nina,
who started it all
—R.P.

For Isaac,
Sherri, and Meggie
—R.W.A.

~~~~~~~~~~~~~~~~~~

Published in 1991 by Magi Publications,
in association with Star Books International, 55 Crowland Avenue, Hayes, Middx UB3 4JP
First published in 1990 by Four Winds Press, Macmillan Publishing Company, New York, USA

Printed and bound in Hong Kong

Text copyright © 1990 by Robin Pulver
Illustrations copyright © 1990 by R.W. Alley

ISBN 1 85430 241 8

When Mrs Toggle's children arrived at school in the morning, they changed in the hall from their boots to their shoes.

When the bell rang, they picked up their boots and bags and marched along to their room.

They stuffed boots and bags into their cubbyholes and hung up their coats. Then they sat down at their desks.

"Good morning, Mrs Toggle," the children said in their best morning voices.

"Good morning, class," said Mrs Toggle in an unusually grumpy voice.

Then the children noticed that Mrs Toggle was still wearing her coat—the big, puffy, fuchsia-coloured one that she got for Christmas.

"Mrs Toggle!" yelled Joey. "You forgot to take your coat off!"

"I didn't forget," said Mrs Toggle uncomfortably. "I can't take it off because the zip is stuck. I'm afraid it's going to be a long, hot day."

"How did the zip get stuck?" Nina asked.

Mrs Toggle fanned her face. "How does any zip get stuck? First a tiny bit of cloth gets caught in it. Then you pull and keep pulling a little too hard. And before you know it, you're completely trapped."

The children gathered around Mrs Toggle's desk to see for themselves.

"Yes," said Joey, "that zip *is* definitely stuck." The others nodded.

"What's worse," said Mrs Toggle, "is that the thingamajig's gone."

"The what?" said the children.

"The thingamajig—that you pull the zip up and down with. Mine is lost."

"Oh," groaned the children. They all thought happily about their own coats hanging on their hooks with their zips open and their thingamajigs still in place.

"Maybe we can help," said Caroline.

"It's worth a try," said Mrs Toggle.

Mrs Toggle braced her feet on the floor. She leaned forward in her chair and held out her arms. Some children grabbed one sleeve; some, the other sleeve. Paul and Nina grabbed fistfuls of collar.

"Now!" yelled Mrs Toggle, and everybody pulled.

And everybody landed, with thuds and bumps, in a heap on the floor. Mrs Toggle's collar was as far as her nose, but no further than that.

Paul wanted to get busy learning the times tables. "Mrs Toggle," he said, "let's go to the nurse's room. Maybe Mrs Schott can help you."

So Mrs Toggle and the children trudged along to see Mrs Schott, the school nurse.

When Mrs Schott saw Mrs Toggle's hot, red face, she reached for the thermometer and popped it into Mrs Toggle's mouth.

Mrs Toggle shook her head. "Addon avva tepashhur!"

"Don't talk with a thermometer in your mouth," said Mrs Schott sternly. "I'll telephone your mother."

"Addon livwif ma mudder," mumbled Mrs Toggle.

"Mouth closed!" ordered Mrs Schott.

Nina spoke up. "She's not sick. Mrs Toggle is hot because she can't get her coat off. The zip's stuck, and the thingamajig is lost."

"Then we must pull it off," said Mrs Schott.

"Oh, we tried that," Paul said.

"This time we'll add a bandage," the nurse answered. "Bandages make boo-boos better. But first, Mrs Toggle, you must take that thermometer out of your mouth!"

Mrs Schott stuck a bandage on the zip where the thingamajig was supposed to be. Then she pulled, and the children pulled, and they all ended up with thuds, bumps and bangs on the floor of Mrs Schott's room.

Mrs Toggle's collar was as far as her nose, but no further than that.

Mrs Schott shook her head. "I'll call the Head. He'll know what to do with you."

The Head, Mr Stickler, left important matters on his desk to hurry to the nurse's room.

Mr Stickler frowned when he saw Mrs Toggle. "Mrs Toggle, it's against school rules to wear your coat all day."

"I am sorry," said Mrs Toggle, "but I can't take my coat off. The zip is stuck."

"Tell him about the thingamajig!" said Nina.

"The what?" Mr Stickler asked.

"You know," said Paul, "the whatsit."

"The doodah," said Caroline.

"The whatchamacallit," said Joey.

"My pupils are right," said Mrs Toggle. "The thingamajig is missing from my zip."

The Head frowned again. "Mrs Toggle," he said, "in my job I have learned that if you want to get out of a tight spot, you must follow the rules.

"Pay attention, children," he said. "Make two straight lines. One line pull on the right arm, the other line pull on the left. Mrs Schott, you be responsible for the collar. I shall pull on Mrs Toggle's feet."

"We've tried that," said Joey.
"Pulling doesn't work," Nina agreed.
"Did you make straight lines?" asked Mr Stickler.
"That's the rule. Stay in straight lines. Now, ready … steady … pull!"

The children and Mrs Schott pulled in one direction. Mr Stickler pulled in the other direction. Mrs Toggle tried to make herself small and wriggly. But with thuds, bumps, bangs, and a kerplop, they all ended up on the floor again.

Mrs Toggle's collar was as far as her nose, but no further than that.

Mr Stickler said, "Enough of this. We don't want holes in the school floor just because of Mrs Toggle's zip. I'm calling the caretaker. I'm afraid he'll have to cut this coat off!"

"No!" yelled the children, and Mrs Toggle cried, "Never!"

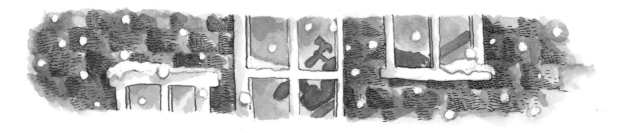

The caretaker, Mr Abel, arrived wearing his big work apron. Tools bulged in every pocket. He looked at Mrs Toggle in her coat. "Is the building too cold for you?" he asked kindly. "Maybe the thermostat's off. I'll go and check."

"Wait!" said Mr Stickler.

"Look," said Caroline, "Mrs Toggle can't get her coat off because the zip's stuck."

"Yes," the Head said, "and there's a problem with the thingamajig."

Mr Abel listened carefully. "Mmm," he said. "I can see the puller is gone."

"The what?" said the children and Mrs Toggle and the nurse and the Head all together.

"I said, the puller's gone. Don't worry, I've seen worse."

Mr Abel pulled a pair of long-nose pliers out of one huge apron pocket. He used the pliers to loosen the grip of the zip's metal teeth on the shiny, fuchsia-coloured lining of Mrs Toggle's coat.

Gently, with his large fingers, Mr Abel eased the lining away from the teeth. Then he slid the zip down, down, down. It opened completely. Mr Abel helped Mrs Toggle off with her coat.

A happy smile spread over Mrs Toggle's face. Mrs Schott and Mrs Stickler and the children cheered.

"You should get a new puller for that zip before you zip it up again," said the caretaker.

"I certainly will, Mr Abel," said Mrs Toggle. "I am eternally grateful to you."

The Head went back to important matters. Mrs Schott rushed off to check a child for chicken pox. Mrs Toggle and the children traipsed back to their room to tackle the times tables.

Mr Abel pulled a small pad from his huge apron pocket and wrote himself a reminder: "Remember to look up 'thingamajig' in the dictionary."